My House

Lisa Desimini

My House

Henry Holt and Company · New York

For my friends

dave & heidi shannon

dave riccieri

a true story

sara schwartz

ann farrell

frank gargiulo

natalie & brian schaefer

victoria raymond

allison koch

keller & scott bryan

matt mahurin

katherine & sean murphy

My house wakes up at daybreak,

and makes pictures in the sky.

It gets dressed in the fall,

and gets lost in the snow.

It comes alive in the spring

and shimmers and sizzles on hot summer days.

It floats in the fog,

stands strong in the wind,

and is safe in a storm.

After the rain, my house lies in puddles.

In the afternoon light I have two houses.

When the sun is low, my house wears a hat.

Sometimes it is crowned by clouds.

My house is quiet and still at dusk,

then disappears into the night

filled with dreams.

Henry Holt and Company, Inc.
Publishers since 1866
115 West 18th Street
New York, New York 10011

Library of Congress Cataloging-in-Publication Data: Desimini, Lisa. My house/by Lisa Desimini. *Summary:* Describes a house in different weather and light conditions. [1. Dwellings—Fiction.] I. Title. PZ7.D4505My 1994 [E]—dc20 93-49549 ISBN 0-8050-3144-8/First Edition—1994/Printed in the United States of America on acid-free paper. ∞

1 3 5 7 9 10 8 6 4 2